EVER CLEVER EVA

EVER CLEVER EVA

Andrew Fusek Peters

Illustrated by Teresa Murfin

A & C Black • London

For my mother, who fist told me the tale
of Ever Clever Eva

White Wolves Series Consultant: Sue Ellis,
Centre for Literacy in Primary Education

This book can be used in the White Wolves Guided Reading
programme for independent readers in Year 5

ISBN 978-0-7136-8883-2

A CIP catalogue for this book is available from the British Library.

This book is produced using paper that is made from wood grown
in managed, sustainable forests. It is natural, renewable and
recyclable. The logging and manufacturing processes conform
to the environmental regulations of the country of origin.

Printed and bound in Great Britain
by CPI Cox & Wyman, Reading, RG1 8EX.

Contents

Chapter One   7

Chapter Two   21

Chapter Three   37

Chapter Four   49

Chapter Five   65

About the Author   79

Author's Note

In my days as a storyteller, I asked my
mother if she knew any folk tales. She
grew up in Prague in the 1930s and this
story was told to her by her nursemaid
and is well known among the Czechs.
The heroine was called Manka, but I
wanted to use my aunt's name to give
the book its title, *Ever Clever Eva*.

Chapter One

Long, long ago in a little village just outside Prague, there lived two brothers.

Master Jan was as rich as a treasure box, but his younger brother Eduard was as poor as a pebble. The poor brother had a young daughter called Eva.

When Eva was 14 years old, her father reluctantly sent her out to work. There was only one job going in town and that was as a goose girl.

This was no easy task, as geese are quite happy to bite the fingers that feed them. Even worse, it meant that Eva had to work for her rich uncle, who was well known for his meanness.

Eva moved into her uncle's farm.

Every day, she rose at dawn to feed and water the cackling geese. After that, her chores were endless – washing dirty clothes, scrubbing floors, dusting surfaces, polishing old bits of brass and cooking the food.

Each night, after eating the leftovers tossed away by her uncle, she fell asleep exhausted, but at least she knew the money would help her family.

As was the custom, at the end of

the year, Eva went before Master Jan and put out her hand.

"I hope you've found my work satisfactory?"

Master Jan rubbed his moustache. "It'll do, I suppose," he grumbled. "The geese haven't died, and you haven't managed to poison my food."

He turned back to his papers and ignored Eva's outstretched hand.

"I would like to be paid my wages for the last year," said Eva.

Master Jan looked up, surprised. "You would, would you? Hmmm…" He stuck his finger in his ear and dug around as if he might find the money in there. "Tell you what. I've got a lovely calf in the barn. When she's fully grown, she will be yours to sell at the market. How does that sound?"

Eva smiled. It was a good deal. Now she woke up every morning with a spring in her step and a smile that sat like the sun on her face. The geese were spoiled and the floors scrubbed until they shone.

The time rushed by. All the while, Eva watched the calf grow fatter.

After nearly two years, she stood before Master Jan once again.

"Dear uncle, I hope you've found my work satisfactory?"

Master Jan rubbed his moustache. "It'll do, I suppose," he grumbled.

"The geese haven't keeled over, and you haven't managed to infect my food with some rare disease."

"Good!" said Eva. "I would now like the cow you promised, as I intend to take it to market this afternoon."

As she spoke, Eva looked forward to seeing the look on her father's face when she brought home the money. There might even be some left over, once the rent was paid, to treat them all to a feast and some new clothes.

Eva's daydreams were interrupted.

"Cow? What cow would that be?" The look of surprise on her uncle's lying face was cunningly innocent. "Why would I give you a cow? You should be grateful that I feed you and give you a warm bed to sleep in!"

The drafty hay barn was hardly the warmest bedroom in the world and the leftovers that Eva was lucky to scavenge did not make her grateful.

In fact, she was fuming. Her uncle had gone back on his word! What should she do? There was no point staying at the farm and working for nothing.

In a moment, Eva made up her mind. She ran from the room, down the stairs, out of the yard and away from the farm until at last she reached her family's tiny cottage. There, she threw her arms round her father and sobbed out the whole sorry story.

Eva's father was furious. He stomped up the hill to his brother's farm and ran up the stairs of the house two at a time. Before Master Jan could utter a word, his brother grabbed him by the ear and pulled hard.

"You're coming with me, you
dishonest excuse for a scoundrel!"

And with that, Eduard dragged
him out of the farm and into the centre
of Prague, right to the courthouse.
The judge was sitting there in his
purple robes on a big chair.

Both brothers told their story.

Master Jan made it sound like Eva was a lazy good-for-nothing with an eye on his hard-won fortune.

Eduard made his daughter sound like a saint who had suffered severe hardship.

The judge was an honest-minded man, but he didn't know who to believe. He sat back on his chair and considered the situation and finally he came up with a solution that he thought rather clever. He decided the only way to solve the problem was to set a riddle and see who could give the right answer.

"I want you both to go home

tonight," he told them, "then come back to my courtroom tomorrow morning with the answers to these three questions: What is sharpest? What is sweetest? What is richest?" He pointed to Master Jan. "And don't forget to bring the cow!"

Both men walked home feeling very gloomy. Master Jan had no idea of the answers. He might be rich, but he was also as thick as a dumpling. He begged his wife to help him.

His wife, who had put up with him for too many years, took out a turnip and slapped him hard. "You potato head!" she said. "How did I ever manage to fall in love with you?

The answer is easy as peas! What is sharpest is the tooth of our black dog! What is sweetest is our store of honey up in the loft! And what is richest is, of course, the box of gold hidden in the cellar! Now go away and make sure you remember to get the answer right in the morning."

Master Jan felt so relieved, he could almost have kissed his clever wife. He smiled a silly smile and slept well that night.

When Eduard returned home, he told his daughter all about the riddle. He had no idea of the answer, and his heart was as heavy as a stone.

"Don't you worry yourself, dear

father," sang the girl. "Go to sleep now and, in the morning, I promise to give you the answers to the riddle!"

That night, in her sleep, Eva's brain churned round and round until the answers floated into her mind.

When the day turned over the sky like a page in a book, Eva woke her father and whispered quietly in his ear. His gloomy face brightened like the sun. It looked like they were in with a chance after all!

Chapter Two

The next day dawned bright and clear. After listening to his daughter, Eduard went to the courthouse. On the way, he met his brother, who was leading the cow on a rope.

Master Jan looked down his nose. "Good morning, Eduard! I don't know why you bothered coming today. You know you're going to lose."

But Eduard had put up with his brother's taunts since they were little.

Silence, for now, was the best answer.

They finally arrived at the courthouse, where a servant took them before the judge.

The judge did not want to offend the wealthiest inhabitant of the district, so he asked Master Jan to speak first.

The rich brother stood up and took a deep breath. This was going to be a walkover. "I have the correct answer, my lord!"

"You have? Let's hear it, then!"

Master Jan rattled off the responses to the three riddles. "Of course, what is sharpest are the teeth of our black dog, ready to bite anyone who comes near. What is sweetest is our honey, stored in the loft. What is richest," and here Master Jan smiled, as if he had come up with the answer, "is the huge casket of gold that we keep hidden in the cellar of our house!"

The judge nodded gravely as Master Jan waited for justice to be served in his favour.

"Wrong!" announced the judge.

Master Jan couldn't believe his ears. His face went as red as a beetroot. His greedy eyes bulged. This was impossible! He opened his chubby mouth to complain, but the judge raised his hand for silence.

Now it was the turn of Eva's father, who was feeling quite nervous.

Eduard said a little prayer and opened his mouth. "What is sharpest," he said quietly, "is the eye that sees the truth. What is sweetest is dreams at the end of a long and worry-filled day. And what is richest is, of course, the fruits of the earth that can feed us long after all the gold has melted away!"

The judge sat back in his chair and beamed. This was more like it! "Absolutely right," he said. "That settles the case. I do believe that the cow now belongs to your daughter."

Master Jan jumped up. "But... But..."

"I will hear no appeals. Unless, that is, you fancy spending a few days in the lock-up for questioning my decision?"

The judge waited for an answer, but Jan's shoulders drooped as he shook his head in defeat.

Jan stomped out of court, leaving his precious cow in the hands of his now not-so-poor brother.

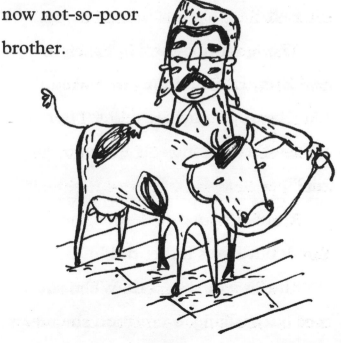

Eduard made to go but, before he could, he was summoned before the judge's bench. There was a puzzled look on the official's face.

"Tell me, and tell me truthfully," the judge asked. "Did you come up with the answer to the riddles all by yourself?"

"No, your honour, it was my daughter, Eva," Eduard answered.

"Hmm…" said the judge. "Let me ask another question. Is your daughter fair?"

It was a strange question to be asked, but Eva's father did his best. "Put it this way, my lord. When she goes out walking, every man she meets

has their eyes stolen, their lips silenced
and their hearts thumping like a gong."

The judge's eyes lit up. "Well, well
well! Then I would be very interested
in meeting this clever, and beautiful,
daughter of yours," he pronounced.
"Tell her, if you will, to come to me
neither by day nor by night, neither
dressed nor undressed, neither shod nor
unshod, neither riding a horse nor
walking by foot!"

Eduard's face dropped. This was a
tall order. He had won the case thanks
to his daughter, but now the judge had
set an even harder riddle. The thought of
it made his head spin. He trailed home
with the cow and put it to pasture.

"Why the glum face?" said Eva. "You've brought home the cow, which shows you got the answer right."

"True, my fair one. The only problem is that afterwards the judge started asking about you!"

"Why would he be interested in me?"

"I told him that you came up with the answer and then I had to admit that you were a ravishing beauty!"

Eva was pleased. "You think so?" she said, as she twirled a bit of her long, curly hair in her fingers.

"You know I do, and now the judge does, too. He has summoned you to appear before him, but that's just the start of it." Eduard recounted the judge's orders. "He insists that you come to him neither during the day or night. Not only that, but you musn't be dressed or undressed. Nor can you be shod or unshod. And the final command is the most ridiculous. You have to arrive without walking or riding a horse!" Her father finished speaking and shook his head in despair.

"Father, have I ever told you that you worry too much? The judge might be intelligent, but I think he's finally met his match!" Eva had a determined look on her face. "Leave it to me!"

At two o'clock the following morning, Eva woke up. Instead of putting on clothes, she jumped into a potato sack. On one foot she put a shoe but no stocking. On the other foot, a stocking but no shoe. Then she clambered onto the back of the cow she had rightly earned, and ambled into town.

As the cow clattered up the cobbled streets, the clock struck three. It was the twilight time, when neither day nor night can decide who will win the fight to cover the sky. Eva reached the judge's house and ordered the cow to stop. The cow gave a huge bellow, which echoed up and down the narrow alley and shook the windows.

Up above, the shutters were thrown wide. The rudely awoken judge leaned

out of the window. When he saw a girl
wearing a sack, sitting on the back of
a cow, he burst out laughing.

"My dear young woman, you are
so clever and, even wearing a sack,
your beauty is beyond compare!"

The judge was an impatient and decisive man. Without even blowing her a kiss, he asked Eva the biggest and most difficult question of her life: "Please will you marry me?"

Eva looked him up and down from head to toe, thought for a second that he was not too bad-looking and said, "Why not!"

"I am so glad to hear it." The judge smiled as he leaned out of the window. "But you must promise me one thing before we take the plunge."

"And what's that?" Eva asked, with a sweet smile on her moony face.

"You must *never* interfere in my work as judge of this town."

"I promise with all my heart,"
Eva replied, though she did wonder if
it was a dangerous promise to make.

All good things came to pass, and
within three months they were married
in the town church. The feasting and
drinking went on all night and both
Eva and the judge danced their knitted
socks off. And so it was that after the
honeymoon, Eva moved into the judge's
house in Prague, with her cow, which
she put in the backyard.

Chapter Three

Eva and the judge were very happy together for a year and a day. On that day, Eva was out shopping in the market, when she saw a man sitting in a doorway, looking very sad and sorry for himself.

"My dear fellow, why the frown on your face?" she asked.

The man looked up and, seeing Eva's pretty features, managed the briefest glimmer of a smile.

"Good day, my lady. I would not dream to cast a shadow on your morning with my tale of woe."

"Try me," said Eva. "I'm all ears."

"Oh, all right then."

The man told her about himself. He was the poor but proud owner of a young mare. His richer brother owned a stallion that he kept in a neighbouring field. One night, the frisky stallion had leapt the fence and a few months later, the mare gave birth to a foal. The poor man insisted the foal belonged to him, but so did his rich brother. They took the case before the judge of the town, who was normally known for his wisdom in such circumstances.

"Yes, he is…" interrupted Eva. "Do go on."

But in this instance, the judge had come down on the side of the rich brother. The poor man wondered if it was something to do with his brother's offer to contribute to the courthouse funds.

"You mean, a bribe!" Eva was shocked.

The poor man nodded his head.

This was not on. Her husband had behaved like a fool and Eva decided action was needed.

"I want you to do something for me," she demanded. "And it might serve your purpose well."

"What's the point?" wailed the poor man.

"Oh, stop snivelling!" said Eva. "Just do as I say. My husband, the very judge you are speaking about, goes hunting on Skarman Hill just outside Prague every Saturday morning. I would like you to be there an hour before him. Take a fishing rod with you."

"A fishing rod?" The poor man looked puzzled.

"Exactly. As my husband rides by, cast your line into the grass."

The man looked at Eva strangely. "My lady, have you been drinking?"

"No!" said Eva, shocked. "Let me

explain. My husband, being the rational fellow he is, will no doubt stop and say that you are mad."

"I *am* mad, to be listening to you, my lady. Fishing in the grass! Whatever next?"

Eva smiled triumphantly. "And that's my point. When he says that you are mad, you can tell him that you're not as mad as he who believes that a stallion can give birth to a foal!"

The poor man looked at Eva again. "Wow! That *is* clever. I am sorry for ever doubting you, my lady."

"Thank you," said Eva. "But promise me you won't tell my husband who gave you this idea."

The poor man gave his thanks and went on his way. The next morning, he rose early and took his fishing rod up into the meadow on top of Skarman Hill. He began to cast about for green fish, blue fish and flower fish, but apart from a few shoals of drifting mist, he didn't catch a thing.

After a while, the judge came riding by, off on his way to the hunt. When he saw a man fishing where there was no water, he shouted out, "You there, what are you doing?"

"Fishing in the grass!" replied the poor man, with a grin as big as his face.

"Fishing in the grass? Have you gone completely mad?" said the judge.

"Not as mad as he who believes that a stallion can give birth to a foal!" replied the poor man.

The judge went as red as a tomato. His eyes bulged. He opened his mouth in shock. "Very clever indeed! You shall have your foal after all. But tell me, and tell me truthfully, or I shall be forced to throw you in jail," he threatened. "Was it you who thought of this idea?"

The poor man shook with fear. He would have to break his promise.

"No, sir, it was your wife Eva who told me..."

"Right then," said the judge, gloomily, and rode off in a rage. When he reached his house, he kicked the door open and shouted for his wife.

Eva came walking down the stairs and looked him in the eye.

The judge pointed his finger at her. "Remember what you promised me before we were married?"

"Of course I do." Eva knew what he was going to say.

"You have interfered in my work and broken your promise," he shouted angrily. "You must leave this house tomorrow morning, never to return!"

"Look…" Eva argued. "I know what I said, but you have to admit you were wrong about the foal and the stallion. Surely justice is more important than a mere word?"

"Oh, stop trying to convince me with your cleverness," the judge ranted. He knew that Eva was right, but he was too proud to admit it. "You broke your promise and must accept the consequences."

Eva felt the tears sprout from her eyes and roll down her face. She tried to wipe her cheeks as she turned away from the husband she loved.

"But," the judge carried on, "as a gesture of goodwill, I will allow you to take with you the one thing that is dearest to you. Now, choose wisely!" And with that, the judge stomped off to his study and slammed the door with an almighty bang.

Chapter Four

Eva felt alone, more alone than she had been in all her life. Her husband's last words ran through her head. But, as the tears dried on her face, an idea began to form.

"Yes," she murmured. "That is it!"

Putting on a sorrowful face, she knocked quietly on the door to her husband's study.

"What is it?" growled the judge.

Eva slipped into the room.

"My lord, seeing as I am to leave you in the morning, will you allow me to cook you one last meal tonight? Tomorrow I will decide what to take with me, the thing I hold most dear."

The judge felt bad for his earlier words. But there would be no appeal. The case was closed. "Yes, let us eat together and talk of better times. And in the morning, I shall bid you goodbye."

Eva scurried out of the study, trying to hide the smile on her face. She ran down to the kitchen and began to prepare the judge's favourite food.

Two hours later, a rich smell wafted through the house. The judge's nose began to twitch. "Ah, what a scent!"

Then he frowned. He would miss his wife's cooking.

The table was laid with the finest family silver, and Eva poured a glass of their best wine.

The judge sat down as Eva served him from two steaming tureens.

"Oh! It's my favourite! Pork in cream and paprika sauce, with plenty of caraway seed dumplings to soak up the gravy!"

As was the Czech custom, they both ate a slice of bread with a sprinkling of salt. Then prayers were said and the judge tucked in.

They talked about the happy times they'd shared and Eva made sure the judge's glass was kept full. A pleasant hour passed and the judge felt a little merry. I almost wish I could go back on my word, he thought to himself, but that would not do for a judge!

Meanwhile, Eva ate lightly and drank little, all the better to keep a clear head for the evening before her.

She cleared the plates and stoked
the fire, insisting that the judge take
the most comfortable seat.

As he settled himself in front of the
flames, it was the time for Eva to put
her plan into action.

"My lord," she announced. "I hope
you are comfortable?"

"I am indeed. I hope you are not
trying to win me back by showing me
how well looked after I am?"

"I wouldn't dream of it," said Eva,
innocently. "I merely wanted our last
night together to be one that you
remember fondly. Now, I would like
to tell you a story, if I may?"

"Oh, wonderful!" sighed the contented judge. "My mother used to tell me tales to help me sleep at night."

Eva nodded. That was her *exact* intention.

"Will it entertain me?"

"I should certainly think so. Sit back, close your eyes and let me take you away."

The judge did as he was told and Eva began her tale.

There once was a woman who had no work, which was a bit of a problem as she wanted to be rich. Well, it just so happened, as these things do, that one day there was a knock on the door. Who was it then, do you think? None other

than Death himself. How could you tell?
He was skinny, real skinny, so skinny he
had no skin. Just a lot of bone beneath
his black suit. His face looked a bit pale,
and he didn't have any eyes. It was
definitely Death. No doubt about it.

The judge interrupted. "Isn't this a
rather gloomy tale?"

"Don't worry, my dear, even Death,
the judge of us all, meets his match
some time," said Eva.

"Very well then. Continue!"

Eva put another log on the fire and
carried on with the story.

Death said to the woman, "You want
to be rich? No problem, my dear lady!
Just call yourself a doctor. And when you

go to visit the poor patients, don't worry,
I'll be there. Here's the trick. If I am
standing at the head of the bed, that
patient will get better simply by you
laying your soft hand on their head…
But, if I am standing at the foot of the
bed? Forget it, that patient is mine until
the end of time!"

Death smiled while he was talking.
He had a lot of teeth and the woman
wondered for a second if talking without
a tongue or lips was the only trick Death
had up his sleeve. Finally, she agreed
to the plan, though she questioned why
Death was trying to help her. Still, it was
something to keep her busy. She made
some calling cards and gave them out,

*waiting for the summons. And the call
came, one dark night. She was asked out
to the poorest area of the city and came
to a one-roomed shack. A ragged, worried
mother pushed her inside. The rotten
door gave way to cold, damp interior.
A young, skinny man lay in the single
bed, eyes closed, waiting to die.*

*But guess who was standing at the
head of the bed? It was Death! No doubt
about it! Quick as a thought, the woman
put her hand on the boy's head. He
opened his eyes, and the mother jumped
for joy. Death smiled and the woman
went home.*

*Next day, the call came again. It was
a rich man's house this time, in the best*

part of town. There were plenty of rooms, each with its own fireplace and floors strewn with rugs so thick you could sleep on them. She was led up the stairs and into the richly decorated room, to see the man's wife not looking well at all. Her eyes were closed and she was waiting to die.

Can you guess who was standing
at the head of the bed? It was Death.
No doubt about it! Quick as an eel, the
woman put her hand on the wife's head.
She opened her eyes, and the rich man
jumped for joy. Then he gave her a bag
of silver. Death smiled and the woman
went home.

Word about the miracle doctor spread
like Chinese whispers. And every time she
went to a house, guess who was standing
at the head of the bed? It was Death.
No doubt about it! Soon, the woman was
rich as rich can be and richer still. The
only thing missing in her life was a little
bit of love.

"A little bit of love... Hmmm!"

sighed the judge as his eyelids almost began to close, despite his best efforts to keep them open. After all, his tummy was full and what with the drink and the fire, he glowed all over like a contented ember.

"Yes!" said Eva, agreeing. "The only thing missing was a little bit of love." And she continued the tale...

The woman, who was rich now, dreamed about the perfect man in her life. But her dream was interrupted by a royal summons. It was the king! No doubt about it!

"My son is ill!" he said in a very royal voice. "All the wise women and wise men in the land have tried their

utmost. Potions, spells, pills and exercises. Nothing has worked, and soon my son shall be nothing also. If you can cure him, his hand shall be yours in marriage, as shall half of my kingdom. But if you cannot," the king thundered, "then you shall return home without that which sits on top of your shoulders — YOUR HEAD!"

Chapter Five

The woman had not a worry in the world. Why, Death always stood at the head of the bed. This would be simple! So she dressed in her finest clothes, dabbed perfume behind each ear and made her way to the castle. The grand gold gates opened before her. She was led through stone corridors wider and longer than rivers, up great stairs of marble until she came to the prince's bedroom, which was large enough to contain a house.

In the centre lay the four-poster bed,
fashioned from four oak trees. The heavy
bed rested on four tiny wheels so it could
be moved for cleaning. The prince was
hidden from view behind curtains of
green velvet. The king drew the curtains
back.

And guess who was standing ... at
the foot of the bed? It was Death. No
doubt about it! And he was smiling a
toothy smile. What could the woman do?
She was in despair. She would lose her
head! She thought and she thought and
she thought, until she had a flash of
inspiration. Quick as a shooting star, she
turned the bed right round, until Death
was standing at the head of the bed.

Before he could say anything, she put her hand on the young man's forehead. The prince opened his eyes. It was love at first sight.

"Oh, very clever. Very clever indeed!" mumbled the judge, who could feel little waves of sleep creeping closer and closer like a tide.

"I think so, too!" smiled Eva with a glint in her eye. "But wait a minute, all is not won yet!" She carried on...

Things happened very fast. The woman married the prince that night, with a big feast and lots of drinking and dancing. The new princess was as happy as the sun. Morning came and they rode off out of the castle as man and wife.

Now guess who came swooping out of the sky? It was Death. No doubt about it! He grabbed the princess before she could cry, "Wait a second!" and whipped her up into the sky, past the clouds, by the sun, through the stars, down the Milky Way, into a darkness so black there was nothing to be seen, until at last they came to a door.

"After you, my lady!" Death bowed as she opened the door. Behind, was a vast room, full of flickering oil lamps. "These are all the lives of all the people in all the universe. When the oil runs out, they will die and it's my job to tend the lamps." He reached up onto one shelf and pulled out two lamps. Each of them had various marks on them for the different stages of life from IMMORTAL down to VERY OLD AND NOT MUCH TIME LEFT. But the lamp he held in his hand only said FIVE MINUTES TO GO. "This, my dear lady, is your lamp. I am ever so sorry!"

What could the woman do? She was in despair. She was about to lose her life! She thought and she thought and she thought, until she had a flash of inspiration. Quick as lightning, she turned to Death.

"Dear Death, seeing as I am to die in only five minutes, maybe I could tell you a story to pass the time?" she smiled sweetly, and Death agreed it would be a pleasant way to pass the time. He settled his bony frame into an old armchair stuffed with human hair and the woman began to tell him a tale all about two brothers, one rich and one poor. The poor brother had a daughter who went to work for her rich uncle as a goose girl...

But Death was not a very good listener. He began to yawn politely and then found himself falling into a deep, deep sleep. By the end of the tale, Death was snoring away, the breath whistling through his pearly white teeth.

This was just what the young woman wanted. She ran to the oil jar, filled up her and her husband's lamps right to the top where it was marked IMMORTAL.

Death slept on as she crept out of the room, through the darkness so dark there was nothing to be seen, down the Milky Way, through the stars, by the sun, past the clouds, into the sky and back onto the horse she had left only a second before. The prince had not even noticed she had gone. And guess what? They rode off into the new day, and lived happily ever after. Definitely in love. No doubt about it!"

Eva looked up and saw that her husband, like Death in the tale she had told, was also now snoring and slumped in his chair like a sack of potatoes. It was exactly as she had planned. Maybe *her* story could have a happy ending, too.

She summoned the servants, who carried the master of the house up to bed. Once he was under the covers, Eva told them what she had in mind.

"You're not serious, mistress?" said the servants.

"Oh, I am. It's a matter of life and ... death! Now will you help me, or not?"

The servants whispered among themselves for a few seconds. "We are acting against our master's wishes, but we also agree it might be the best solution. You can count on us!"

"Thank you," said Eva

Each one of them lifted a corner of the bed and carried it gently out of

the room, down the stairs, through the
front door, along the cobbled streets,
into the fields and finally up to the
cottage where Eva's father was waiting
with a hug for his daughter.

The morning washed across the sky like a wave in the sea. The judge stretched, yawned and finally opened his eyes. At the foot of the bed stood Eva. Definitely Eva. No doubt about it!

"Where am I?" demanded the judge, feeling rather confused and with a big thumping pain in his head.

"You are in my house, in my bedroom!" said Eva.

"But I told you to leave me! The last thing I remember is sitting by the fire and you telling me some story about a very intelligent woman..."

"And you also said, kind husband, before I left, that I could take the one thing with me that I held most dear.

And that one thing, of course, is *you*!"
she beamed.

The judge frowned for a second. His
face turned as red as a poppy in bloom.
Then he realised how clever his wife
really was and burst out laughing.
"How right you are, and how stupid
and proud I have been. You really are
the wisest woman in the whole world,
even wiser than the woman who tricked
Death!" said the judge, "And I hope
you will forgive me."

Eva smiled and said, "As long as
you promise never to interfere in our
love for each other!"

The judge had to agree. No doubt
about it!

After they kissed and made up, the judge had one more thing to say.

"My dear Eva, I think you're much better at telling right from wrong than me. Therefore, from this day onwards, I shall give up sitting in the courthouse and you shall be the judge of this city!"

Her husband had spoken well, for it came to pass that Eva was a wonderful judge and everyone in Prague was very happy.

And as for Eva and her beloved husband? Well, they lived cleverly everly after.

About the Author

Andrew Fusek Peters has written over 70 books for children. When he isn't stuck behind his computer, you can find him doing author visits all over the country with his didgeridoo, juggling balls and skateboard.

His latest books include the thrilling new series *Skateboard Detectives*. For A&C Black he has written *The Story Thief* and *Ever Clever Eva*. You can find out more about him and his work at www.tallpoet.com

Year 5

Myths, Legends and Traditional Stories

The Path of Finn McCool • Sally Prue

The Barber's Clever Wife • Narinder Dhami

Taliesin • Maggie Pearson

Playscripts

Fool's Gold • David Calcutt

Time Switch • Steve Barlow and Steve Skidmore

Let's Go to London! • Kaye Umansky

Stories From Different Cultures

Granny Ting Ting • Patrice Lawrence

Ever Clever Eva • Andrew Fusek Peters

Bamba Beach • Pratima Mitchell